AF472314

The Poetry

of José Gorostiza

American English Versions of the Spanish

by Robert Klein Engler

Alphabeta Press,
Des Plaines, IL

e: RKleinEngler@aol.com

CONTENTS

for Professor John W. Kronik,
formerly at the University of Illinois, Urbana,
who taught me how.

ACKNOWLEDGMENTS

My version of "Del Poema Frustrado" first appeared in *Colombia Magazine* and *The International Poetry Review.*

My translation of "Fireflies" first appeared in the *Mid-American Review.*

The poems translated in this book are taken from José Gorostiza's *Poesia,* Fondo De Cultura Economica, Av. de la Universidad, 975; 03100, México, D.F., 1964.

Critical consideration of Gorostiza's work may be found in:

Debicki, Andrew P., *La Poesía de José Gorostiza,* México: Ediciones de Andrea, 1962.

Gelpí, Juan, *Enunciación y dependencia en José Gorostiza: Estudio de un máscara poetica,* Mexico, Universidad Autónoma de México, 1984.

Ramírez, Edelmira, *José Gorostiza: Poesia y Poetica,* Colleción Archivos, Madrid, Spain, 1988.

A valuable guide for part of my work was Laura Villaseñor, whose book *Death without End* was published by the University of Texas in 1969.

This is growing old.
You've played your cards.
The sky is white and cold
And poems come hard.

--RKE

The Life and Poetry of José Gorostiza

Cada quien persigue el destino desea para sí.

--José Gorostiza

I first became aware of José Gorostiza's poetry on New Year's Day, 1984. I was sitting on a bench along the Paseo de Reforma in Mexico City. It was early in the morning. Christopher was still asleep back at our hotel room. The festive atmosphere of New Year's Eve had given way to a cool and bright dawn. Across the street I could see a plywood barricade that had gone up temporarily around a construction site. The boards were covered with graffiti. On one of them, a tagger had written some verses by José Gorostiza. The writing was signed by: "The Committee for the Defense of the Language." I was struck by the poem, and the next day I went to a bookstore in the Zona Rosa and bought a thin volume of Gorostiza's complete works. I have been translating his writing since then.

José Gorostiza was born in Villahermosa, Mexico in 1901 and died at Mexico City in 1973. He taught Mexican literature in the National Preparatory School from 1930 to 1931 and general literature in 1933. He became an honorary professor of Spanish American literature in the University of Mexico and a consultant to the Mexican Embassy in Havana.

Gorostiza has been described as a delicate and scholarly poet whose early work goes back to the seventeenth-century Spanish lyric. As a young man, he had been associated with the *Ulysses* group of Mexican poets. He also belonged to a group of poets called the *Contemporáneos*. The *Contemporáneos* rejected the stale Modernismo of the time in favor of individual fulfillment for its members. Villaurrutia called it a "Group of Solitudes." This group included such poets as Jaime Torres Bodet and

Xavier Villaurrutia. Gorostiza dedicated many poems to members of this group, but as time passed, he managed to escape the gravity of any group or school and set his own poetic course. Though berated in their time, the *Contemporáneos* have exerted a lasting influence on Mexican poetry.

Of all the members of the *Contemporáneos,* Gorostiza's poetry is the most taught, distilled and personal. His poetry is highly refined and very subjective and for some seems to capture in Spanish what T.S. Eliot was attempting to do in English. Gorostiza is also noted for his poetic craftsmanship. All this praise might seems unusual, in that his fame rests solely on two books, *Canciones para cantar en las barcas,* Songs to Sing in Boats (1925) and *Muerte sin fin,* Eternal Death (1939). In 1969 he published the poems in *Del Poema Frustrado.* Salvador Novo believes Gorostiza's work will perhaps be the most lasting of the *Contemporáneos.* He writes, "His influence on Octavio Paz is perceptible to such a degree that Paz could well be described as the successor to the author of *Muerte sin fin.*"

Gorostiza's poetry is subtle and authentic and his lyrical quality along with the intensity of *Muerte sin fin* assures him a central place in modern Mexican poetry. In his book, *The Labyrinth of Solitude,* Octavio Paz says that, "The poem ... (Death Without End) ... is perhaps the best evidence we have in Latin America of a truly modern consciousness, one that is turned in upon itself, imprisoned in its own blinding clarity." Some themes to look for in Gorostiza's work are: the importance of the sea and water, perhaps reminiscent of Greek poetry and Homer; a lament over the absence of love, and the eternal presence of death.

The Poetry of José Gorostiza

(For Doña Elvira Alcalá de Gorostiza, my mother)

I. Some Notes About Poetry

PROLOGUE

The poet has ideas about poetry in which he attempts to relate what exists in his consciousness to the mysterious substance he tries to write about. From what I am able to observe, these ideas are very precise, each one in its own place. They are as precise as those ideas that an artisan has about the qualities of his material or the abilities of his tools. But because of faults of articulation and method, it is not possible to string them together into a body of doctrine. Nevertheless, it is possible to offer them in a state of nature, to offer them as personal impressions that are able to slightly penetrate the enigma of poetry. Most often when we offer these personal impressions, they describe an image of the personality of the poet rather than poetry itself.

The poet is not able, without handing over his position to philosophy, to apply all the rigors of thought to an analysis of poetry. The poet simply knows poetry and loves it. He walks like a blind man that pursues what he loves. He recognizes poetry in each one of it apparitions and captures it, finally, at times, in an exact net of luminous words, with his heart pounding.

Poetry is no different in essence than a game of hide-and-seek in which the poet both describes and denounces poetry. Between poetry and the writer, as between lovers, all that exists is the joy of playing the game.

POETIC SUBSTANCE

I like to think of poetry not as something that happens within a man, something that is inherent in him, natural to his humanity, but rather as something that has its own existence in the external world. In this way I contemplate it as something like a wide horizon far from me, or as one looking at the sky from the false hypothesis that the earth is suspended in it, suspended in the middle of a deep night. The truth, for the eyes, is in the universe that surges around us. For a poet, poetry exists by its own virtue, everywhere, wherever the poet turns to look for it.

Thus I imagine a poetic substance, similar to the behavior of light, that reveals hues and colors in all that it bathes. Poetry is not essential to sound, color or form, just as light is not the object that it illuminates, nevertheless, when it lights up an object of art--as in painting or sculpture, in a musical composition or a poem--it quickly announces its presence by its brightness and its supernatural transparency that it carries.

There are various works of art in which poetry does not play a part. The Parthenon in its majesty dwarfs and humbles. Its architecture is grandiose and exquisite. The Taj Mahal, on the other hand, when it appears reflected in the mirror of its pools, can be viewed as flooded with an incontrovertible poetic inspiration.

The poetic substances, according to my imagination, are often derived from theological notions learnt in our early youth, and are always with us. We are able to meet them in whatever corner of time and space, for one finds them better hidden than manifest in the objects in which they live. The recollection of emotion that their discovery produces and signals, as in the meeting of Orestes and Electra, is the meeting of poetry with the poet.

DEFINITIONS

It happens, although not frequently, that the individual artist--let's say a painter or musician--takes advantage of the resources of another artist who is not a poet in order to make poetry. This occurrence is almost always involuntary and, when the association produced is a consequence of a natural movement of creative inspiration, the effect is one of complete abundance. The paintings of Beato Angélico come to mind. The unity of his religious emotion and poetic sense translates into a series of small paintings, each one equal to the stanzas of the *Spiritual Canticles* of San Juan de la Cruz.

The word is, above all, the proper terrain of the poet and the necessary instrument for poetry's proper expression. I would like to know why this is so, if someone is capable of explaining it to me, but then I would ignore that explanation, and in my ignorance say to myself,--what a supreme evasion to offer green grapes instead of wine--the interest of the poet is not in "why," but in "how." How does one make the transition from words to poetry? The poet, like everyone else, is the prisoner of the denotations that general usage coin, yet it seems he alone is able to facilitate the exchange of such delicate transactions.

From my point of view, in my poetry and the poetry of others, I have come to believe (permit me to support myself on air again) that poetry, upon penetrating words, takes them apart, opens them up as if they were a cocoon, to let all their shades of meaning come out. Beneath the spell of poetry, words become transparent and we are allowed a glimpse, although from far away, of the walls around words becoming transparent. We see not only what is said but what is silent. We note that there are doors and windows opening into all directions of the understanding, and that between word and word there are secret corridors and drawbridges. We cross, in our imagination, toward dank dungeons, and airy, elevated galleries that we don't have in our own castles. Poetry has brought to light the immensity of other worlds that circle our world.

A good friend of mine asked me once, "What is poetry?" I remained perplexed. I don't know what poetry is. I never knew and perhaps never will. Over time I have read much about poetry, from Plato to Valéry, but I am afraid that I have forgotten it all. Nevertheless, I answered that poetry for me is an investigation into certain essences--love, life, death, God--that produce in its effect a breakage of language is such a way as to make language more transparent, that we are able to see through language to these essences.

Before similar concepts just as vague, no one is able to escape from being depressed and frustrated--such is the invisible matter we are trying to capture--that I already feel inclined to correct myself and say that poetry is a speculation, a game with mirrors, in which words, put next to each other, reflect off each other into infinity. They then recombine into a world of pure images where the poet takes possession of the powers hidden in us and establishes contact with that person or thing beyond.

But, as you have already noticed, this second definition is, although said in other terms, just the same as the first. Nor is it able to stand alone. Like a mumbling invalid, it doesn't make much sense.

TRAVELING WITHOUT MOVING

Lao-Tse said, "Without going out your door, you are able to know the whole world, without looking out your window you are able to see the road to heaven. The more you travel the less you may know. You are often able, without moving, to learn, without looking to see, and without doing, to create."

Behold how in a few choice words, the force of the human spirit, unmovable, crucified in a profound loneliness, is able to amass treasures of wisdom and arrive at the road to salvation. One of these roads is poetry. Thanks to poetry we are able to create without doing, we may stay at home and nevertheless voyage.

PARENTHESIZES

In my time I have heard people talk a bit about the supposed unpopularity of poetry. They are in the habit of attributing this unpopularity to diverse causes. Chief among them is the obscurity of many modern compositions. They seem impossible to understand by people without poetic sensibilities. I doubt if poetry was very popular in past times either, when the bards sung of heroic deeds at banquets and Ulysses was moved to cry when hearing of his own misfortunes. The people who gathered around such a table--almost always the well provided table of the royal house--were without a doubt people of long ancestry. They had a principal interest in the cult of poetry, since poetry was made up of the historical and religious traditions they held as important and the nursery of all their human knowledge.

In our language, since the days in which, as the result of an intense research into the roles of classical antiquity, the "high priesthood" of the poet colors the art of poetry, poetry itself is turned into a thing of worship. The poet is born, but once born, he writes. From this point of view, poetry, like all the rest of the artistic and scientific disciplines of our time, becomes an object of devotion by a small minority that believe in it, or that simply possess the necessary preparation to enjoy its pleasures.

There is nothing abnormal in this, but in the special case of poetry it happens that its vehicle, our language, is also the popular instrument of communication between people, and while not all sensitive persons paint, it is not difficult to admit, if we think about it, that they all speak. There are also some, possessors of a respectable degree of education, who say that they enjoy the latest Stravinsky or that they prefer the first paintings by Dalí, or, better yet, that they like these works of art while confessing to have no interest in understanding them. But when they gather together to hear a piece by a major poet, if they don't understand it, they feel it as a personal insult on them by the author. "What a fraud," they say, "How can he trick us with words like that!"

POETRY AND SONG

If poetry were not an art *sui generis*, an art having its own existence, and if it were necessary to establish its kinship in respect to other disciplines, I would dare to say (in these times) that poetry is music and, in more specific terms, song. In this respect I am not far removed from the popular notion of poetry. History shows us that poetry in its infancy was a sister to the singer, and later on, when it was able to walk on its own feet, without the direct support of music, it still owed much to music. By working with language, the poet has adapted to it the conditions of music. Rhythm, accent, pauses, harmony, in poetry all owe their importance to their musical roots.

The poets of my group--the "group without a group"-- that was lead by Xavier Villaurrutia were pleased to discover the individual talents of each other and were somewhat strangers to the generation that proceeded us. But events did not exactly follow our coming together. Between 1920-25, and the passing of Rubén Darío's stentorian voice, Modernism filled the atmosphere with a powerful resonance. In truth, the Modernists were the ones who had been our closest models. Poets like Nevro, González Martínez or López Velarde were influential. Our group had been born for poetry beneath the awesome sign of Modernism. And what was it, in our worship of form, but nothing more than a orgy of musicality?

A movement of reaction, in the sense of opposition, then began. My generation marched, as a question of principal, with a certain disdain towards the resources of prose that we thought sacrilegious. But it was not them, imbued as it was with the taste of beautiful forms, who put that disdain far behind. Where better to observe this reaction than in contemporary poetry, although not so much in Mexico but in other Spanish speaking countries, where Spanish poetry is decanted into indigenous cups. The forms of the sixteenth century seem to have been stamped forever in our literature with the unmistakable seal of its classical inheritance.

By reason of this--and this is the fact I wish to underline--we confront a contemporary posture that desires, if not to liberate poetry from music, then at lest to resist serving it. The poetry of the young does not need music to empower it or enslave it, it flees from the operatic and declamatory and takes refuge in a species of stammering and vague rhythms, in which they introduce here and there a perfect hendecasyllable (a line of verse having eleven syllables) or an involuntary rhyme. Such it seems as if in the splendor of a crystalline atmosphere, the poet feels surrounded by an excessive fragrance that prevents him from filling his lungs. From this moment one comes to see as pure superficiality all that poetry has elaborated in the language in order to realize itself.

We know that there is much sincerity and truth contained in the attitude that offers us a poetry stripped of all unnecessary cosmetics. Not only this, we know this attitude is not gifted with a timid voice either. Poetry will surely recover from this experience. It is helpful, however, to remember that nothing exists in total freedom. Everything is subject to degrees, and liberty consists in nothing more than the sense proper proportion within an established order. The rules of chess are not applicable to the juggler, but where they do apply, they draw a zone where they unroll toward infinite possibilities.

The affinity between music and poetry is congenital. In any given moment this is realized up front or in the background, but it will always be so because this affinity is not situated in language, not in the austere arsenal of rhetoric, that goes in and out of fashion, but in the human voice, the voice that poetry borrows to make it spoken, to make it realize its full perfection.

The difference between poetry and prose consists in that while one asks of the reader to borrow his eyes, the other ask that the read hand over his voice. Each poet has his own personal style (at times this is an indication of his aesthetic philosophy) to speak his poems. One sings, another recites, some mutter while others sob. No one is confined to only reading. Poetry is entrusted to whoever speaks the poem. In the act of speaking the voice imitates singing and leaves the throat vibrating with the pulse of life that only a voice can give it-- for it happens, my dear friends, just as Venus was born from the waves, so poetry is born from the voice.

THE DEVELOPMENT OF A POEM

Not so long ago, stimulated by a lecture by Veléry, I preoccupied myself as he did with discovering the laws that governed the creation and ending of a poem, in order to make use of them. The classical poem, and here one can consider nothing more or less than a sonnet, comes to be seen as the standard by which one measures poetry. The difficulty is not in knowing how one begins a poem. Every poet has at hand his first line. The difficulty is in knowing how a poem develops and how it ends. This is the thing. There is undoubtedly a variety of steps which are not easy to recall, but two or three of them--the most common--come to mind.

In the first, which I will call plastic development, the poem grows like a painting in the sense of filling up a surface. We have a plain before us, brilliant and direct, and we have a scale of perspective in which various shades of motives ascend. Plastic development is limited in that the poem must conform to the space the author gives it. It is finite, because there, within that space, it exhausts itself and ends. If he's lucky, the poet can retouch it, if he wishes, but he cannot continue to make it something else. Given its system of interior life, the poem remains in front of us like a painting, open to our capacity for contemplation.

A poem may also have a dynamic development. It advances or ascends with a dynamic progress. It goes forward to a climax and proceeds rapidly to this termination. The poet has to weigh beforehand the path of the poem that corresponds to the path of a projectile. By this method the possibilities of growth result in something that is inexhaustible. The poem is able to prolong itself indefinitely, because it accumulate verses or establishes a vicious circle, like in those stories that never end. It is the poet, with his sense of proportion that brings it to an end.

Finally, we have a poem in which we never notice growth. From the first to last lines, it grows and takes on an insensible body like the development of a life, like a fruit or a flower. It develops without strain, naturally. Its length, its proportion, all is dictated by its vital breath. A madrigal by Cetina was produced this way. It could not have been more succinct or more explicit and there it remains, within its small body of the poem, overflowing with its precious childhood.

CONSTRUCTION IN POETRY

In his *Defense of Poetry,* Shelley observes that "The parts of a composition are capable of being poetic without the composition, as a whole, being a poem." Nor is nothing more certain, as things go, that it is possible to have a house in which each room was admirable, but all of them taken together are not able to be united into what makes up a livable house. Is this not a question that no one doubts? If a poem shows itself to us as the English poet suggests, we would be in the presence of a failed work, and the failure would be nothing more that the fact that the poem was a failed piece of architecture. Poetry and architecture are equal to poetry and music, they are all nursed by the same mother.

Actually, the poet is not in the habit of proposing problems of construction. From time to time--nowadays even less--he uses certain elements of the tradition and builds with them, quartet by quartet or lyric by lyric, finger by finger if you will, as a building of shadows is built. If the unity of the interior is profound, it is thanks to the builder and not to the strength of the materials employed. The sonnet, for example, provides an occasion to build a poem according to a gracious model. In the case of greater constructions, like the vast poems of another age, nowadays, an occasion hardly arises. I wish to say, and am not able to keep it silent, that I feel this loss of form as an enormous loss to poetry.

We are living under the reign of the lyric. Poetry has abandoned a great part of its traditional territory which it used to dominate in other times. The dialogue, description, the narrative, these and other poetic forms, which were combined in books like *El Libro de Buen Amor* by Arcipreste de Hita, for example, all have been taken over by the resources of the theater and the novel.

Within the lyric, as we see it diminished today, it seems that the only cause capable of undoing a poem is the element of autobiography. The shock that an event produces in the poet when falling upon something from his personal life, translates itself, converted into images, to an emanation or flood of poetry; but this is not a poem, because this word "poem" implies intelligent organization of the poetic material. Thirty or forty compositions (in which one can recognize always the content of authentic poetry) is in the habit of forming, one after the other, what the public calls "a book of verse." (What a horrible expression: a book of verse!) And in such a book one may find a certain uniformity of emotion and style, and from one poem to the other, qualities and elements that link the poems and that give the sensation of an invisible continuity; but the book does not show, all at once, the unity of construction that please us in a real book. The sum of thirty musical moments will never make a symphony.

Every day history proceeds toward a future where any notion of compassion seems alien. Nothing would be more foolish than to ask that poetry be today as it was yesterday. Likewise, we have to imagine what it will be like in the future to try to see how it is today. Nor is it absurd in our time, the dawning of the atomic age, to imagine a world without poetry, a world of "experts" where poetry is outlawed as a scandalous manifestation of primitive men. But above all, the question remains, "Would it require too much for the parts of a composition to be poetic and at the same time all of them taken together result also in a poem?"

THE QUESTION OF ENVIRONMENT

When we think about poetry as a revelation of the beautiful it is not difficult to conclude, even if we are not a very profound thinker, that one thing is certain; that is the beauty manifest by poetry is not taken from the external world, borrowed as it were from external objects, it is not the natural beauty of a cloud or a flower. It is, on the other hand, an artificial beauty, a poetic beauty, that poetry borrows from the rose and from the cloud, temporarily, for its own ends.

This was not always understood, nor is it understood by some now. Nevertheless, the transparency of such a correct distinction between beauty and poetry is equal to the distinction between human beings and things. For the ordinary reader--and likewise for some poets--poetry is like a secret tunnel that allows us to escape from our prisons, to escape from the ugliness and horror of our surroundings, toward infinite pastures illuminated by the splendor of the beautiful. Reason helps them to make this escape, but I am afraid that they are mistaken when they reason that it is a necessary conclusion that poetry ought to capture and exhibit the magnificence of the world.

So also has poetry been associated in the course of its history--in contrast to the contemporary conception of prose--with the use of an elegant language in which only certain precious materials (silks, gold, diamonds) seem able to offer to the imagination points of terrestrial support. Nevertheless, this is also not correct, and like the error that sees poetry coming from the fountain of beauty, it wants to situate poetry within a special atmosphere, as special environment, in a special scene that the taste of the moment considers appropriate. There have been many such "poetic environments," such as the pastoral that the Spanish Golden Age of poetry admired and imported from the Classical pastoral, or the oriental environment from the Turkish salon, that the Romantic poets loved so much. They are all false, however, like the paper of a stage scene that are useless for reality. This kind of atmosphere adds nothing to the essential beauty of poetry.

Above all, the tendency to elaborate a "poetic environment" lasts into our time and does not lack those supporters who are sincerely convinced that poetry gains something if it presents or represents the exterior signs of our epoch. Perhaps those that believe such do not bear in mind that an appearance of actuality is, like any other appearance, external to nature. It is the same as poetry that is made completely of essence and interiority.

We ought to admit, nevertheless, by elemental confidence in the sincerity of our human fictions, that no one looks for error to begin with, but that we accidentally fall into error in our haste to get to the truth. Perhaps the man of today, stacked up in sprawling cities by the millions, is not like the men of other times. Men today do not live as individuals in constant contact with nature. The sky does not appear as a great stretch of blue these days to the eyes of a city dweller. As a prisoner in his room, feed up with silence and hungry for communication, man has been converted to an island surrounded by other other islands on all sides. His gardens are now the flowers designed into the carpet, his bird songs are broadcast over the radio, his spring breezes are provided by an electric fan, his love is the muttering of the woman who sews in the corner of a flat. Poetry is not needed by this man in order to enrich his environment with beauty. Strictly speaking, if it were certain that poetry was nothing more than a reflection of beauty, he ought to flee to it from all his surrounding miseries and ugliness. Nevertheless, this man needs poetry, a poetry that comes to his life like a cool breeze and enriches it, that saves him from the great dangers that threaten him and that give his dignity to walk with pride among his fellow men.

A MAN OF GOD

One works in common with others to write a poem, even though every poet is alone in his ivory tower. The poem does not result from a sudden encounter with poetry. There have been poets that, throughout their whole work, do nothing more than perfect a single poem. Likewise there are poems that, in the delicate process of their maturation, ought to consume the labors of many poets. The history of poetry--like history in general--suggests the image of a current, a river whose waves emerge from the wider body of water, then fall back again and dissolve.

Because poetry, although it may sound incredible, is tainted with life, it has to die also. It is killed by the very instruments that give it form, words, styles, sentiments and tastes, poetic schools. Nothing ages as rapidly, with the exception of a flower, as a poem ages. The poet will make it last one day more or less, according to his ability to take away the force of time. A poem's destiny is transitory, like all things, and it will disperse itself in the depths of popular wisdom. I have heard common people, void of all culture, repeating thoughts of Shakespeare as if they were their own. Or better, a poem may be relegated to the shelves of libraries like a object of archeology, where it will remain for inspection by the curious and for study and inspiration of other poets.

All these things the poet need not know, and if he does, he doesn't have to remember them. An historical consciousness will kill the muse in him. The poet does not have to produce like an opera sings, who, along with thousands of other singers, exploits the same song. He has to feel what is unique in a world that is a desert. He has to consider for the first time what it is like to gave names to things. He ought to be sure that he posses a message that only he knows how to translate, at the right time, with the correct, eternal word.

The mission of the poet is an infinitely delicate one. We ought to shield it from innocent pride; we ought to defend it, if necessary, with the whip of our childish vanity. After all, neither the individuality nor the length of a work ought to matter much as a concern among readers. In poetry as in a miracle, what has to happen, what is important is intensity. No one but the Supreme Being, far from us, who we do not know, can sustain in the air for a few seconds the perfume of a violet. The poet, similar to the Supreme, sustains the miracle of poetry for a fraction of a fraction. Among all people, a poet is one of the elected few who we can justly call a man of God.

II. Songs to Sing in Boats

1. Who Will Buy an Orange for Me?

For Carlos Pellicer

Who will buy an orange for me,
an orange for consolation,
ripe from the orange tree--
bright with circulation?

Salt of the sea upon my lips,
salt of the sea within my veins--
is this the salary for my pains?

Who might give to me
their lips to kiss--
or share a tender kernel
from the harvest that I miss?

No one asks to drink my juice,
so I may never know
if blood in me is tied or loose,
or if I come or go.

Are ships lost upon the sea,
like clouds above the bay,
are we so lost and gone astray?

And since you never ask for me
I have no heart to mention.
Who will buy an orange for me--
a gift for consolation?

2. The Sea Shore

It is neither water nor sand
the wide sea shore.

The tide steals out
and then restores,
yet never forms itself
against the shore.

In and out, to rest
in shallow pools,
the water and the land
compose a border without rules.

All things secret,
gentle, in rapport
come together
like the wavering shore.

Likewise are the lips
I dream to kiss--
neither water or sand,
that shore of happiness.

Alone upon the sea
I find myself a thing apart,
naked on a desert,
with breath my counterpart.

And then I realize--
why say more--
it is neither water nor sand
the wide sea shore.

3. The Sea Celebrates

For Carlos Pellicer

We go to look for banana leaves,
to gather and make a weave.

How happy is the sea.

We go down the road looking for them,
asking the grass to lift its hem.

How happy is the sea.

Because the moon (ending five years of grief)
turns white, blue, red, the color of a leaf.

How happy is the sea.

The moon accepts the counsel of the sea
Perfume of sun and fog are her degree.

How happy is the sea.

Seven stalks of spikenard will I separate
for my lover to appreciate.

How happy is the sea.

Seven stalks of spikenard, as perfume,
I carry to my lover's room.

How happy is the sea.

Life, spent like coins, I know you well,
but for my lover, who can tell.

How happy is the sea.

Life, I say, spent from my treasury,
Don't come back counterfeit to me.

How happy is the sea.

III. Other Poems

A Dim Awareness

For Bernardo Ortiz de Montellano

An old man smokes his tobacco
in a blistered, walnut pipe--
the clouds of afternoon hang low
with yellow memories of love once ripe.

The old man nods and sleeps.
How sad to see him foolishly wait
like the broken watch he keeps
or a forgotten calendar with yesterday's date.

It's quiet here, an auspicious device
for half remembering things,
like the inappropriate advice
ventriloquists repeat with puppet strings.

The simple landscape washes clean
beneath the sunset's faded glow,
his broken watch reflects a sheen
like thumbed mahogany or worn intaglio.

A meager recollection of antique
smoke trails from the walnut pipe,
listen, the yellow shutters creek
with rusted memories of love once ripe.

The House of Silence

The house of silence,
with its hood of rotted tiles,
is upright by a corner of the mountain.
It seems so peaceful
that it hardly rattles with the sound
of wind in the nearby trees,
where a bird's nest hangs by a dream.

Perhaps no one inhabits it,
or wishes to,
perhaps most men have never seen it,
yet its deep heart beats
with a profound throb of resignation,
when the mutter of wind
or a quivering of blood wounds it.

I imagine, in the house of silence,
a sun lit patio,
made ragged by grass
that gnaws at the flagstones,
and a wall of chipped paint
about to fall from the torrential rains.

And in the deep blue nights
I think about the trouble it foretells,
I hear it spill its small sounds,
a stammering of stars off the stone bench,
almost imperceptible, yet contained,
I hear its paternal weeping
of three thousand years.

Sickness Unto Death

Within the ample silence of a moment
a vague fear appears.
Perhaps the door will open for no reason
and you will see a far vision
as if the soul were a bay window.

In the hall a caged bird sings.
The faucet drip, drip, drips.

Perhaps the high curtains pretend
to fold themselves, ambassadors
of a mysterious hand,
and the uncertain murmur
in the eyes of the sick man
cause a trail of tears in the corridor.

In his opaque eyes, dying,
there is no hope for tomorrow.
Only one complaint flows
from bloodless lips of sorrow.

A nun thumbs her rosary
and remembers the crucifixion,
but a strange fear admits
the shadows of vespers.
In the pendulum of waiting
one see the collapse of love.

Perhaps the door opens for no reason.
In the hall a caged bird sings,
the faucet drip, drip, drips...

Fisherman of the Moon

When you see red lanterns on the shore,
my fisherman with dark eyes,
lower your black nets once more
into the sea that tempts with lullabies.

At night the sea reflects a sheet of ebony.
The lips of waves are touched with gold
beneath the moon, just like a subtle filigree
within the eyes of one you wish to hold.

Do not cast for the fish of the moon,
my fisherman, the waters of the gulf
will salt your bones too soon.

Do not search for the morning star,
my fisherman, the waters let it go,
for like a sleepwalker gone afar,
stars come and go and tilt to vertigo.

How fragile the currents and pools
that play the eddies of illusion,
like dreams of light that seduce fools,
they rise and fall in black confusion.

Do not cast for the fish of the moon,
my fisherman, the waters of the gulf
will salt your bones too soon.

With fearful eyes you stab the sea,
but it absorbs those silver hooks
the way your beard absorbs your tears--
a spear to water is like eyes to books.

Do not cast for the fish of the moon,
my fisherman, the waters of the gulf
will salt your bones too soon.

Nocturne

For Eduardo Luquín

This moonless night with constant rains
is a perfect time to tell the stories of pilgrims
that tramp the mud of long roads.
Blinded by the bright storm the sky contains,
they nevertheless advance a faithful requiem
to the small jewels of morning that distance them.

This night without stars brings a knock
at my door from a weary traveler, and though
I would deny him my money, the simple art
of my table, and the peace of my patio, he can unlock
my will and enters my house and my vigilant heart,
troubling me even if I stay apart.

Illuminated by the shinning mirror of rain,
when every field was a silver membrane,
waving his white hands like lilies,
he told me a simple and charming refrain.
From his lips, hidden by a yellow beard,
the mortal song of the mermaids still adhered.

I was not able to stop him, nor smother
my greeting as he neared my defenseless door.
The black lightning of his eyes testify
to that bit of pride he needs to call me brother.
Those eyes that still retain a little of the summer sky,
against the nets of rain cast out to mystify.

But you, my friend, what noble ecstasy you view,
you never open the door when anxieties shout.
Somehow, you can hid when you hear the snap
of a branch telling you of a melancholy retinue
coming to find the secret balm you keep about--
the oil that seals you from my watery doubt.

Pause I

The sea, the sea.
I think only of it.

I feel it within me,
deep to a fault,

even my thought
has a taste of salt.

Women

For Ciro Méndez

CORDOBA

From my peaceful city I am drawn
to a town of lukewarm sleepiness.
There they know of salt on the lips of dawn.

I carry with me from my valley
a long heartache
as anxious as the transparent sea.

Here the women with pointed breasts
cross the narrow ribbon of streets,
their waist are all a melody suggests.

There was a glow on their warm lashes,
two agates lit their eyes,
and on their lips, sweet poison kisses.

In undulating lines they promenade,
like doves they softly flock
beside the lilacs and the balustrade.

And thus they lived on filtered juice
from apples pressed in paradise,
and scented with the flower of every muse .

By our God I bestow on them
a verse from my transparent
cup like those recited by Hugo.

And they dry my fountain to a drip
for this sweet, languid sample of a kiss
from the delicate cup of adolescent lips.

Córdoba, so much of you I miss:
I promised them the light of sunset
for the languid drop of just a kiss...

And they gave me the sun!

Squall

Night, dark as a womb,
with black clouds and scratched lightning,
whose bright verbs double in the sea.
Minister of silence,
I ask only a small part
of the desolate shore
where I may simply rest
as a dim beacon for sailors.

It ought to be overcast now.
The sea holds back the swift ships.
While you think of the anguish from a star--
a North wind loosens its gold--
I, with no aftertaste of dust from the road,
will think of a happy kiss, mature as wine,
sweet as a breath of wind between my lips.

On the same journey with us
are fellow travelers--
a pale twilight from the moon
and the brief bird of a storm.

One divides traveling into stages:
the aurora borcalis and a handful
of light from the evening star
journey with us on the same path.

Night, my somber mother,
when the dark moment of my storm
arrives, is to be suffered here,
together with the salt water.
If I feel like crying
give me blue thoughts,
and steep my words
in the rush of your high tide.

Light

The day threads itself over the city
into a bleak morning
with broken bones of sunlight.
One would guess it is almost spring,
as burst of sunlight break through clouds.

Light, simple light,
(if it were not light
they would call it a smile)
lightly climbs the walls,
drawing out the delicate illusion
of a soft vine.
It glows, trembling
like a wave, a dance.

And the city, with all its stories,
wakes up to the racket of morning
beneath the rude metal of a church bell,
unwinding in a stammering of color.

Now God puts in place for the length of day
a spice of pain and silver nails of melancholy.

Because clear day light,
upon descending in waves of song,
fires the joy of women
in the gray mirror of the heart.

Only yesterday we saw the moon,
diluted above the high silence
of mountains... only yesterday
we saw it spill itself

in an indulgence of guilty lamps,
and try to skim from our eyelashes
the gold milk of its light.

Elegy

For Ramón López Velarde

Alone, with the painful solitude
of the sea, my golden godmother
went for a walk by the light
of the moon that
shutters her brilliance
like the lid of a skylight in the fog.

Sorrow bloodies my thoughts,
and on my lips, like a black rose,
I had my weeping.

The blue baskets of melancholy
emptied out their delicate folds,
and my sleep suffered
with a moon of long, yellow ships.

The lyres put on mourning, women,
in threads of suspended tears,
cut the aromatic curls of their blond braids.

After breaking the quiet of my evening,
I heard the gray of my anguish
slip down like the leaves
in autumn's red gardens.

Put out the lamps, brothers.
The sweet strings of lutes
no longer move in our hands.
For us the seven virtues have died
putting out the thin lips of morning.
Dear God, place a slow weeping
of woman in the eyes of the sea!

Pause II

The cricket stops.
Silence from a star
answers its music.

It measures
the bright pause
with its watch of sand,

and traces
orbits of gold
in the desolate ether.

Nevertheless, there
are a few who know
there is a music box
singing in the grass.

Aquarium

For Xavier Villaurrutia

The multicolored fish play
where Jenny Lind used to sing.

Jenny was almost a girl
in 1840,
but she had
a ripple of embellished water
in the eternal pool of her song.

New York City was small then.
In the deep blue of midnight
recently washed clothes
hung from the tenements sills
of the fourth floor walkups.

We went to Battery Place--
there, so close--
you could see the salutes
of handkerchiefs
from the passing sailboats.

And the bright smiles
at five in the afternoon,
they were like the glimmering
of fireflies in the street.

Later, when a rainbow of light
was thrown as a scattering of stones
against the horizon,
it looked like a flashing of fish,
white, yellow, red,
and we forget we were on Broadway.
Because Jenny Lind was singing
as water laughing with bubbles,
where multicolored fish play.

Romance

A girl from my town
has eyebrows of gold.
In her naked glance
I see the light of fireflies.

Have you seen the boats
sail away from the shore?

Their juggling lanterns--
green, blue, sepia,
that you looked at
tracing over a blanket of mist--
remind us that they illuminate
something far away.

Have you seen a flight of herons
like arrows in the clouds?

They remind me
of your arms batting the air
when we left the land behind,
and the lilac screen of fog
filled with your goodbyes.

And if you sing--yes, sing--
your voice annuls my absence;

mast, rigging and wind
confound themselves
in such a simple chorus,
in such a solemn manner
that the ringing of a star
would not be more clear.

Robinson and Sinbad,
incorrigibly shipwrecked,
to whom will I be able to confide

my complaint, if not to you?
Maybe I'll be shipwrecked one day.
Reflected in a thread of green water,
the lights of fireflies turn to liquid.

IV. Drawings from a Doorway

Drawings From a Doorway

For Roberto Montenegro

1. Dawn

The territory of the sea
is drawn with blood and madder.
Everything sleeps.
On leaving, the dawn
seems just a bubble above water,
and our lives on land,
a repose of boats hand to hand
tilted on a solitude of sand.

2. Afternoon

What violin?

The waves of afternoon roll in

like the pure songs of women.

3. Nocturne

A silence without regret
fills the inlet.
Perhaps the sun is singing
to itself till morning,
or the moon delights
in a borrowed light,
indifferent to her debt.
Palm trees sweep a wealth of shadows
the way her hands smooth cool pillows.

4. Elegy

Sometimes I would cry

but the sea has salt supply.

5. Little Song

At dawn the boats sail west.
They do not love the landfall,
but only return to rest--
or not at all.

6. The Lighthouse

Blond shepherd of the fishing boats.

7. Prayer

The brown boat of a fisherman
prays when put ashore
weary from rowing,
"My Lord, make for me a door
in the waves of this ocean."

Fireflies

For Enrique Gonzales Rojo

1.

A delicate mist flowers
in the blossoms of the peach tree.
The pink air of evening holds
a subtle taste of spring
that permeates its spice.
Girls with feet like the feathers
of a bird walk among the trees.

Who is looking for fireflies
with their opaque lantern?

2.

Blushed by the wind, you seem
like Lady Yang Kuei-Fei
at the imperial peonies festival.
Like her you played
at being a cloud of far away colors
and the transparent dew of afternoon.

What distance
you have at playing absence!
Just like the charmed fool,
all that remains is a perfume,
loosing itself far from the speechless.

What do you look for so far away
on the moon, if not fireflies?

3.

Here I am, drunk again.
Li-Po will return with me
through the watercolors of twilight.
From the distant hills,
lanterns of paper on our shoulders,
will make us look like lost fireflies.

Autumn

For Jaime Torres Bodet

A cold wind scatters a wreckage
of color among the crowd.
Tomorrow is the first day of autumn.
The heart wishes like ghostly swallows
to begin a trip--
our eyes go sick with absence.

Autumn!
Such a golden nakedness.

The mist at daybreak
is like a heron feather against the horizon
that is polished swiftly with a remote wing--
I will have the fragile afternoon
to hear the music of your questions,
to see overhead this endless tenderness.

Autumn!
Such a golden nakedness.

Your silence is as pointed as a mast.
I will act like the whipping wind.
And at the intimate moment of our pause,
in the late autumn afternoon,
no one will know if it was the sail that sang

or the evening wind lately sounding.

Autumn!
Such a golden nakedness.

V. Del Poema Frustrado

Del Poema Frustrado

PRELUDE

Let us begin by invoking the Muses of
Helicon in our song.

-- *Hesiod,* Theogony

That word which never appears
in your language singing of questions,
that faint sound,
which freezes in the air of your voice,
yes, as a breath from a flute freezes
against an air of evaporating windows,
look at it, touch it,
look at it now!
Find it in this anemic mist of magnolias,
in this trivial flowering of fog,
or the shadow of light in the eye of agony,
find it in all the dead locks
anchored to the vacillating sound of waves
that an angel of dreams guards by the window.

What walls of crystal, my love, what walls!
Why such a great silence of water?
That word, yes, that word
that coagulates in the throat
as an amber cry, look at it, touch it,

look at it now.
Know that, from night to night,
decanted in the filter of a jagged silence,
it lingers naked, to say nothing,
wounding and suggesting--
like silence in the after-tick of a clock,
like clarity at the core of a puzzle,
lingering in order to mimic our language--
a silence, that opens to the steps of insomnia
on the sand, to the birds, to clouds,
lingering as dark oracles revolve
in a panorama of prophecy.

Who, if not she, was able to forge
that universal insignia,
born as a hero on her lips?
Look at it, touch it,
burning in an echo of water lilies.
Does not your anguish assume
an innocence like a dumb vine of rhetoric?
Here among lichens
that cut small channels
of finely wrought gold,
is it not thrown out to ring the air
like blank butterflies of frost?

That word, in place of any faith that consumes it
until a transparent destiny,
having escaped from the frozen

arrow of a statue--
soars senseless like a palm tree
and bursts against the sky,
wasting its fire in the pure
delight of fireworks.
That word, yes, that word,
that faint sound,
that drowns itself in the smoke of shadows,
that spins--like a cloud--a cautious gas
from a secret flame, that from which
the aura of a voice splinters,
breathless,
as if it were reflected
in beautiful ulcers of silver,
that which washes its citrus letters
in the foam of sacrificial birds,
that which congeals in a fever,
when not lost in thought to burn
and explode like a fit of tears,
that word, look at it, touch it,
look at it now,
empty of all words,
without voice, without echo,
without a specific object,
understand it the way gray rain
writes lines of water on a wall of glass.

ADAM

Autumn garden from my window--
why are clouds coming from everywhere?
Broken, undone in the prism of rain--
how I remember this Coastal Garden--
how thin are the accumulated remains
of your delicate coins--
God of the arbor; old Apollo
repeating your song;
mistress of the ages;
a fountain with a childish face
of mist that spied on us...
what more are they now than a catalog of ruins?
A verdigris of silence thickens as the water laps.
Perhaps, at a distance of two voices,
the chestnut trees stand in naked dignity--
naked too may be the infamous path
that leads from our happiness.
Or perhaps it is covered with dry leaves
falling from paradise.

MIRROR NO!

Not a mirror--just the luminous,
blank tide rolling in

just the sea breathing in and out--
conforming to the movement of your body--

O, how the high tide burns
like your delicate clarity--

how it brightens--such pure contours--
skin like a flower--distant--

naked and weighted
with the eminent clarity of ice.

Your body conforms with its tenderness
to that to which water conforms--

how the depths return--
with the tide flowing out--

more glass than light--more like your eyes
intent on seeing

specters of colors-- in which
clear--beautiful--wounds bleed.

LESSONS TAUGHT BY THE EYES

Panorama

In the celestial sphere of your dark eyes--
the dead moon is suspended
like the useless watch of a castaway.
At dawn--hardly an atmosphere--
such delicate blue--

it seems so distant--
like the distance between
your thought and your glance away.

Highways

What blue highways
there are in your eyes.
At dawn, deep blue roads,
at noon, so blue
I have to blink--
and at night--dear me--
your eyes are
the phosphorus numbers
on my dark watch dial.

Comparisons

Eyes clear and serene--
so clear one can see the footprint
of a nightingale
in the air--
peaceful
as the eyes of Joseph sleeping
in the well of a tear.
I wish to write a madrigal like Cetina's,
then secretly destroy it.

Stain

Doubt, in her eyes
like a sudden pool--
and the broken horizon at my feet.
Do not throw stones, boy,
against the surface of that pond!

Mask

I am not fooled, flower,
when you appear as fruit
on the bough.
How could you fool me?
By changing your face
you change your age?

The face of tomorrow--
virgin fruit of today--
carries a necessary emptiness
to your eternal eyes
in such measure that the mask
may be none the less your face.

Windows

Is it not also a voyage--to be taken
away by your glance?
Look: the entire city is before us
myopic

with its obscure screen of clouds.
Could it be that we breathe
so close that I stain your eyes?
I wish to write on that window "I love you,"
but then the entire city would know.

Elements

Your eyes were my air
and the air plays upon itself,
over and over.
Your eyes were my air and my fire
and the two play among themselves,
one holding, the other letting go.
Your eyes were my air and my fire,
but also my water,
and the three play among themselves,
holding and consuming.
Because your eyes
were
my water
my fire
and my air,
my soul is filled by your whisper
like a pine tree filled by the wind.
My knotted roots
hold you
because your eyes were
my air

my fire
and my water,
but also
my earth.

PRESENCE AND FUGUE

I

In the sleepless space that separates
the fruit from the flower, the idea
from the act, an isolation germinates,
a death from needles surrounds me.

Feverish, bothersome bee of the flesh--
something drowns in me every second.
It uses my voice, sours what is fresh,
imposes an animal visage on my face.

Are you no longer certain, sweetheart,
you want to destroy this breath
that deserts me with each beat of my heart?

Glacial embrace--now lukewarm ice--
How long, how long can I stand it--
go--go before you die twice.

II

You contain, O form, in the amethyst
wall of incarnate foam that you use,
an obscure appetite for realms of mist
and the feeling of an emerging light.

You are the mistress of a dynamic repose.
It proceeds equally with an *Ave Maria,*
like a sun, with nothing else to consume,
advancing above the silence of Arabia.

Island of the sky, you live in the alkaline
pains of your beautiful shores.
Equal to her, if faithful to your design,

you fill the riverbed with your cold scheme--
to imitate another self, that is born
from the insomnia of my dream.

III

Your destruction gestures in the greed
of my thirst, all feeling is destroyed;
this is not living, saving what you need
from a wealth of trivial gossip.

I look at you already dying in the caress
of your echoes, in that ardent bloom,

that, born in your absence, devours itself
and suggests the radiance of doom.

It isn't her at all, flowing, united to desire.
It is beauty, pure and simple, ungoverned
that assumes her as it consumes itself in fire.

It is only death, an advancing chrome,
that puts in place of her presence
an audacious resume of foam.

IV

Water, do not run from my thirst, stop.
Stop, clear insomnia, that fills the ocean
of this dream without eyelids, that rushes
like the scribbles from a madman's pen.

But it does not want your tender images
that lie about life, no, there are sorrows
much harder, pains that love the depths
from which the fountain shoots its arrows.

Stop, water, your rushing, such haste
blinds my eyes, drowns my song,
set some limit to your rule of waste;

that by your own conception of happiness
you give to me another skin to endure--
O riot of water, serpent, my loneliness.

BOGOTA DECLARATION

You whistled a short tune.
The air descends from black
mountains of storms.
It stumbles in the seamless whiteness
as a ball of light, there in the plaza,
or on the yellow cathedral of oil
that slowly consumes itself,
giving up to dominoes of stars
its stature of a hard flame.
You make the air ring--
it is your flute.
The full moon of your eyes grows larger.
It stamps a rhythm to your swinging arms
that cuts the lines of your walking.
Their noble circles of crystal adjust
and break your pedals and dampers.
Her inscrutable smile drowns me
in the flavor of tea sweetened, little
by little, with the pulp of her lips.
It elevates me, finally, vibrant statue,
to the rigid dance of a sleepless
hammer that beats in my arteries
and will continue to beat--
who knows how long.
I look for love so much that I hurt--
seasick prisoner of the waves.

Behind her silhouette
I see in the window,
the growing sadness of Bogotá covers itself
in the gauzy plumage of drizzle.
Behold our deeds.
In the virtue of our certain lies,
racked with the smoke of your deceit,
behold my voice.
Centered by the ruins of conversations,
my remote voice of balanced words
makes this clear

Declaration II:

You wounded me in the flower of my silence.
The air is bloody from what you broke.
Take it. Take it the way a flute takes breath.
It is a crumb of poetry, nothing more,
a psalm to sing at your wedding.

EPILOGUE

That word which never appears
in your language singing of questions,
that faint sound
which freezes in the air of your voice,
yes, as a breath from flutes,
against an air of evaporating windows,
look at it, yes, touch it, now,

look at it, empty of all words,
without a voice, without an echo,
without language, simply perfect.
Read it as a gray rain writes
lines of water on a wall of glass.

VI. Death Without End

Death Without End

I have counsel and sound wisdom,
I have insight, I have strength

-- Proverbs, 8:14

...then I was beside him, like a master workman;
and I was daily his delight, rejoicing before him always.

-- Proverbs, 8:30

but he who does not find me injures himself;
all who hate me love death.

-- Proverbs, 8:36

Full of myself, caught within my skin
by an unattainable god who smothers me
and perhaps is only imitated
by his brilliant atmosphere of lights
hiding my split consciousness,
my wings broken in splinters of air,
my heavy steps plunged in the mud,
full of myself, stuffed, I discover
in water my amazed image,
an image circulating,
like a chute of angels fallen by
a sheer delight in their bodies,
showing no more than a blank face
half-drowned already, a dying smile,
in a flushed gathering of clouds

and the ominous verses of the sea--
tasting more of salt or lime cliffs
than solitary whispers of foam.
Nevertheless--oh, paradox--molded
by the rigor of clarifying glass,
water takes form.
There it lies, deepens, and arises.
It completes a bitter age of silence,
and a graceful rest of youthful death,
smiling, deflowering far off birds
into disbandment.
Within the strangling crystal net,
as in the water of mirrors,
it beholds itself.
Trapped there, drop by drop,
crying of bubbles and foam in the throat,
what vivid nakedness of water,
what water so wet,
that dreams in its iridescent orb,
singing already a thirst for ridged ice.
Yet also what a blessed glass,
swelling like a seedling star,
lighting up in heroic promise
like breasts inhabited by joy,
to render faithfully
a full flower
of clearness to the water,
a rocket reaching heights
and a window to shinning cries

over that glowing liberty
held in a transparent prisons.

What a fortunate glass it is!
Perhaps this void that draws us out
into islands of echoless monologues,
although we call it God,
is really nothing more than a glass
molding the quick silver soul,
apparent only to us
in an accumulated transparency
dyeing the very idea of God blue.
The very same God
in His timid presence
must spend the blue complexion
and a clear, imponderable innocence
hidden to the eye but fresh to touch,
as in this phantom sea where men,
fish of an airy altitude, breathe.
Yes, He is blue! He must be blue!
A clotted blue of longing,
an embracing tenderness for the creature,
where the spring of its body wells
languidly into stature
between fevers and blisters,
where the hostile river of its consciousness,
spongy, stinging water, spills,
alas, amorphous, to the ground,
where the creature's stubborn footfall

deadens its anger--
where all rounds out like a ledger
and stands up correct like a statue.
What can it be--if not--if not a glass?
Perhaps an incandescent moment
lengthening the furry of its ember,
so much closer to the eternal embrace
and drowning in the time that fills it.
A hollow moment of the spirit
that on any unexpected night,
by chance, and on any ordinary stage--
or the perpetual pacing of the pavement--
in a bar between two bitter drinks,
or on the bald mound of insomnia--
simply happens, ripens, falls
like age, fruit, or catastrophe.
And more that its bed, is not the water,
the glass, a glowing moment, now ripe?
God's hour blooms one day,
it happens, matures, falls,
turns up tomorrow by surprise
in a sterile, unbroken repetition
resembling those electric words--
never understood, always ours--
that elude what memory calls,
but smile at us at every instant
from the empty spaces
of our own deserted monologues.
A glass of time that bolsters us

with its blue buttress of air
and places on us its Mardigras mask,
oh, so perfect
it differs not a hair from us.
But in the small zone of the eye,
with its meager knowledge,
nothing happens, only this light,
this fevered, taut transparency
wrought of utter exaltation
that lets us peer through its clear liquid,
without ever seeing Him,
or what lies hidden behind God:
the inkwell, the chair, the calendar--
all in one blue clamor the secret
of His infantile mechanics--
at the very instant they engage
in the tortured desire of the universe.

But in the notorious zones of the eye
nothing happens, only this light--
ah, Brother Francis, this joy,
unique, smiling clearness of soul!
What pleasure there is in the company
of all the pronouns, muddied before
by the thick, outlawing of egoism--
of me, of Him, of us three--
always three!
While we keenly celebrate this good,
unknowing candor,

this eager innocence of spirit
that sets itself to dream by day
past the ancient absent rose,
and tomorrow's promised fruit,
opaque as the back of a mirror which,
consulting the depths of the image it holds,
only draws from it at last
another mirror in reply.
See with what childlike, fetching gravity
He sorts the worlds from chaos,
adding them up like pearls,
and with a didactic impulse from his finger
cryptically
Snap!
He calls them forth,
pulling from them ribbons of surprise,
stringing them in a symphonic chords,
mingling in them relentless rhythms--
plant, seed, plant--
plant, seed, plant--
their soft breezes, their tender foliage,
their blue moons of barefoot snow,
their quiet copper seas,
and a thousand and one bubbles.
Look how later,
in an unsustainable crescendo
He fires from the sea into the sky
his marvelous shot of flesh,
that in a bird's flight

diminishes even the lofty cloud,
to burst their like a wounded rocket,
and precipitates to the singing stars
a distant dust of feathers.

But even in the marrow of this joy
nothing happens, no,
only a simple dream that roams
all the stations of its route
so lovingly
that it does not even shun hell.
And, with what poison looks,
swollen and still, does it scrutinizes
the track of light, its bright instant
on the skin of a drop of dew;
or conceives the eye
and the oriental oil
that feeds our gaze with its slender light.
It rules the growth of fingernails;
and in the root of words conceals
the speech of philodendrons
and the poem of thorns.
And more-- for in its unholy sky
nothing is crueler than this joy--
it puts its images to the fire,
creates images of false torture:
swells them with passion,
undoes them in a prism of tears,
blinds them with the shine of silk,

bleaches them in the salt of hates,
remembers every scar,
and anguish as dry as the thirst of lime.
And more-- for such perfect, undefinable
malice knows no limit--
it impales the body of its joy
on coarse pins.
It thinks of tumor, ulcer, chancre
soon to festoon the smooth complexion;
and taking the creature in its ethereal hand,
like a flake of warm wax,
He winds, bloats, or rolls it,
and in a glorious twist of irony
closes it tenderly
in the icy arms of fever.

But nothing happens, no,
only this spiral dream
that sees itself in mid-stride,
divines its imminent end,
and then and there prepares
a program for its fatigue,
its merited holiday,
its Sunday off in the country
wearing the cool whiteness of loose shirts.
What a clovered pillow, what a parasol
of mist it uses to cloth the mind,
tasting the honey of its ease.
But rhythm is its norm, the lonely step,

the solitary, sightless round.
So, even from its fatigue it pulls
Slap!
long silver of ribbons of surprise
that in a constant, jealous perishing,
absorbed in dying,
endlessly rend their lovely fabric,
until--child of its own death,
conceived in the desert of its ruins--
it feels its weariness weary,
arises to rest from its rest;
and dreams that its dream begins again,
irresponsible, eternal,
death without end from a determined death,
a heron dream of night-fallen lead,
that changes claws but not the dream,
that changes the image
but not the youth of its daring.

Oh intelligence, solitude in flames,
consuming everything to silence,
like a seed in love
that is able to dream its growing,
to test the glue of its molecules
and the bounds of all its boughs
that will imprison the taste
of forbidden fruit, never outgrowing
its own impassable shell.

O intelligence, solitude in flames,
envisioning all without creating it--
imagine the heat of mud,
its feel of aching potential,
the angry love adorning it
and exalting it higher than wings,
where only the beat of the stars cry,
but breathing in it no breath to rise
and always creating itself anew,
unique in Him, alone in Him,
immaculate,
unspeakable reticence,
loving fear of matter,
angelic egoism that escapes
like a shout of joy over death.
Oh intelligence, wasteland of mirrors!
Frozen breath of petrified roses
at the point of paralyzed time;
sealed pulse;
hermetic system of knots
like a net of trembling arteries,
barely hurrying or slowing
to the force of its delight;
grievous abstinence
that presumes pain but does not believe it,
and leaves on the stair of the ear
the groan of language sounding
without its voice,
absorbing only essence,

and so remaining, angry thrashing,
exquisitely one with its sterile god,
never aligning between them
the dumb weight of flesh,
closing its perfect unity
to the brutal ridicule of that discord
nursed by irreconcilable life and death
following each other
like day and night
encamped together in the cell
as light trapped by twilight.
Solitary, sterile, bitter,
with Him, with me, the three,
single as the glass of water,
absorbing its empty silence
at the lethal edge of the word,
the red cliff of blood.

ALLELUIA! ALLELUIA!

The flower dips its color
in the mirror of a pool,
breeze, perfume, reflection,
so tempting to the fool.

Oh what wonderful delight,
a riot of leafy boughs,
how the air is polished bright
by fingers of the wind.

How delicate the lips of buds,
how full of whispers is a seed,
"I am heliotrope," says one,
"and I, jasmine," "and I, a weed."

And water in the bright lagoon
waits like silver on the moon.

The night has a tree of amber fruit,
the earth has a hue of emerald.

The stubbornness of blood
works with red,
while the dream works in blue,
and joy, another hue.

Love keeps her terrible
hounds of purple,
but also her harvest
and her brilliant birds.

While water in the bright lagoon
waits like silver on the moon.

The apple taste of light,
golden light, and cold,
how easily the sun rises,
like an apple round and gold.

How musty you taste,
sleep like salt upon your lips,
how the hummingbirds
hover for their flowery sips.

Do you think our death tastes
like earth, the spice of clay,
or is it more like honey,
drop by drop, day by day?

And water in the bright lagoon
waits like silver on the moon.

(DANCE)

Poor drops of water come as rain,
holding on to nothing from above,
in a glass of water, in a seed of grain,
poor hands, poor heart, poor love.

In the rigor of the clarifying glass
water takes on its essence.
It carries an Olmec thirst of centuries,
a cold, pointed thirst plowing furrows
in the sluggish dream of earth,
drilling its flowering limbs like caustic blood,
setting them on fire, opening in them
the plagues and ulcers of insomnia.
More love than thirst, and even more than love,

idolatry--a scattering of creatures
stunned before the splendor shot out
by the seed of Olympian thunder,
form in all its beat, spellbound contours.
Idolatry, yes idolatry!
But being a simple psalm, being an ardent
incense of sound, does not suffice.
It also want to hear itself.
Nor is it content to hold mere reflections,
scraps of foam for the of light to nest in.
It wants a bridal bed of shadow too,
an eye to meet the eye that looks at it.
In the lake, the pool, the pond, the cupped hollow
of the hand this ritual of hooks is consummated,
this devilish coupling, chaining love to sin.
Possessed, the water feels the mask of mirrors
furnished by the angles of the glass
congeal upon the clear, featureless face.
At last it has found in its sleepy running
an adequate visage. Now it stands
and faces the world. Now it too, if only
through these slim, prismatic metaphors,
is a burning glass of shapes seen.
The road, the fence, the chestnut trees,
all to die an early, needless
but beautiful death, to enter at your urging
the torment of their own images,
and in the middle of the garden,
beneath the clouds, by the sparse lesson

of poetry, you install a dazzling hell.

But the glass alone is incomplete.
Image of an ill-fated abandonment,
what does it hide in its barren rigors
but this sad, blind clarity,
this groping lucidity?
Leave it there on the table, useless.
Epigram of thorny foam
before an anesthetized listener,
a piercing clamor muzzled by
the stubborn deafness of things,
a mineral flower opening inward
toward its own light,
a narcissistic mirror
draining itself in self-security.
But something is in it, perhaps a soul,
the prophesying instinct of sands,
maybe a blister from the fire,
poisoning it with emptiness.
And this desert longs to be filled up.
In water, in wine, in olive oil
it strings out the code of its desire.
It softens, it stretches, then
suddenly its sober image dims
and, draped in a glimmer,
it flows into tears of light.

But form alone is insufficient.
From its grand, Egyptian throne,
magnanimous, godlike,
starred with dactylic epithets,
it rules with an arrogant, diamond hand.
It is proud of its pompous empire.
In the solemn pituitaries of onyx
does not the spicy aroma of poetry
play at your feet?
It is only illusion, gentle narcotic,
peopling the senses with phantoms.
For, from where pain exhales--
oh dark, festering sun--
its shinning, seductive luster,
from there it posits substance,
its austere pattern barely shaped,
and already is a garden of fossil footsteps,
ringing lantern, red light of alarm
at the crossroads ruling the ways to other forms.
The pink age enameling its skin--
like senility recently born--
creeps inwards through the centuries.
Its prow was always set towards dust.
Air condenses between its pores
like a copious sweat distilling early
an essence of subterranean roses.
The cruel hooks of its death climb
like moss by inaccessible cracks.
Ah, they plague it with cunning bites

and open the wound just at the moment--
look at it in the clock's pendulum,
neat, punctual, precise,
ticking off a link every minute--
when at the infant breath of a blink
the majestic mass of splendid gesture
can fall blow by blow to ash.

Nevertheless--why not?--the dream
has its own form, its corner,
an arid, appleless paradise,
where it can escape from its own face
through the wrinkled features of a specter
engendered by its drowsy rib.
This glass of water is the exact moment.
Transfigured by its bold escape,
it twists the orbit of its fate
and creeps in secret into chaos.
Here in the inhospitable dream
not even rape spoils
the fair pearl of its womb,
nor does the wooing flute of Don Juan
whisper its lustful serenade.
The dream is cruel,
it pricks, gnaws, burns, it bleeds and aches.
It offers us no medicine.
In the deaf hammers pounding it,
form takes relish in the ulcer
and the dark delight of nightfall.

The raw mother of that infant death
feeds in the accumulated ruins.
It longs for its foundation to drown
beneath its feet, numbed
by the heavy torpor of mud.
It hears the thunder of the landslide's roar,
feels its matter spill into an acid
itch of ants, and floats already weightless,
dissolving in a limp silence.
Then through a wind of walking mirrors--
intangible with tattered sails--
the airy theory of a cloud appears.

In a choking crystal net
water finds its form,
drinks in the measure of the glass,
so that it too is transformed in the tremor
of the strangled, voiceless liquid
marking the icy pulse of the current.
But the glass in turn surrenders
to the formlessness of water;
because form itself is in the ridged glass
sustaining the anger of its rigor
in the water of agitated foam,
like a positive omen of repose.
It is apart from the shaft of water--
for only an instant--
the briefest, endless trace of undoing,
when form's own essence

yields to its death's resolve and lets
itself be drawn down, clouds above,
into the tortured vortex where
every being folds again
into the primal torpor
to build the stairs of nothingness.
Then it is that the stars grow black.
They have returned the sleepless dart
into the velvet quiver of night.

For in the long instant of undoing,
when every being folds again
into the primal torpor
and on the arrogant fire of form,
devoured by its death--
eyes, fingers, lips, bodiless
flames of the hellish conflagration--
man smothers with his bare hands
in a black taste of bitter earth
the fair hymns and hoarse dirges
in which he sang of beauty.
Among the drums and sneezed words
and the slender cymbals freeing to the air
their swallows of ringing brass--
every dirge and hymn praising
the seafaring red rose
that circumnavigates the garden,
its sails filled with fragrance,
and the sickly, rusty twilight,

poppy of the wounded air
pricked on the prongs of a bird's trill,
and the feverish star, lily of chills,
dot over the "i" of night,
and the red calyx of firm nipples,
the pomegranate's only flower
on the aching peak of desire,
and the pleasant mandrake dream
growing in the daily ruins--
ah, all the glory of beauty
and the radiant love that binds it all
with orbits of magnetic rapture.

Because the sonorous drum
and the bright clap
of cymbals dispel at the height of song
and drown in a taste of bitter earth
when man finds in his silence,
so his fair language parches,
and is clotted in his throat,
spent of meaning.
Yes, his aerial tongue of colors
that boasts its faithful nuance
in the stricken smoke of its rust
or in the sun of its warm vermilions;
that which talks in the longing of the lip,
like a slow-opening rose in love;
that chisels its dove like jealousy
and tempers its savage whips;

that bounces in its fall
with a noisy rhythm of foam;
that prolongs the insomnia of its embers
in the withered ashes of the ear;
that darkly crawls
and, furiously, plunges to the word of gall,
the one-eyed phrase of poison,
that shapes our smoke of sacrifice
into columns of spiral rhythms.
Yes, all the bold language of man
smothers, jumbled, in the throat,
leaves nothing of its first grace,
but the horror of a dry well,
that supports a toothless grin of agony.

For man finds in silence
that his glib language dries up
at the very moment of undoing,
when all the fish,
swimming in cautious circles
like small scaled stars,
through the countless undersea night,
when all the fish,
with the Ulysses salmon of return
and the Apollonian dolphin, fish of gods,
retrace their way toward algae;
when the tiger that milks
the chastity of moss
with secret, leather paws

and the sparks of the pursued stag,
and the bleating lamb with wig's wool,
and the Babylonian lion pinning
for the alabaster of the friezes--
eternal flowers of blood
on the immemorial stem of the species--
when all of them begin the return
to their mute vegetable slumbers,
when the treble lark
dissolves in the mist of dawn;
when all the birds,
the lone owl in his mask of phosphorous,
measuring the shadows, the swallow
of Hebraic characters, and the little sparrow,
hungry in the snow--when all the birds
fade into the coiled, reptilian night,
when, finally, all that walks or crawls
and all that flies or swims
shrink into the flapping of butterflies,
retreat into their own beginnings
and the fatal genesis of beginning,
until their echo repeat themselves
in the first, dark silence.

For all the beautiful beings that cross through
the ancient slumber of the earth--
ghosts of flesh and blood straying
on the screen of its polluted dream--
when all surrender to a frenzy of death,

when the willow accumulates its tears
to weave the stuff of delirium
in which--you, I, we... suddenly,
from weaving ill-matched names,
only the tight trunk remains,
naked of prayer before its star;
when naked too are blushing,
and the trembling, silver bearded poplar
or the murmuring eucalyptus,
layers of leaves, a whirlpool of green,
chasing and losing itself in clouds,
and also the cherry and the peach
in their mad, adolescent effusion;
and the frightful anguish of the cotton tree,
and everything that is born of roots,
from the heroic oak
to the cold mint of cruel April,
when the bark of all humble plants
draws in the presumptuous boughs,
hides within their knotty roots
and in the bitter cells of their roots,
a light, seized by a crazy growth,
unfolds into the seed,
until it halts, stilled, by darkness.
Oh cemetery of carved roses
in the frozen gardens of stone.

Because from the heroic oak
to the cold mint of cruel April,

everything that is born of roots
fixes its paralytic stem
in the white gardens of stone.
When the ruby of angelic pride
and the wrathful diamond
retorting its flash at light,
as well as the blue-eyed Aryan sapphire
and the rustic emerald flooded
in the May of its vital chlorophyll,
follows one by one the delirious stones,
with their lovely sisters of ashes,
turquoise, lapis lazuli, alabaster,--
but also imprisoned gold
and truth-telling silver,
honest nightingale of metals,
drowning in the well of song.
When the precious stones and exquisite metals
return to their subterranean nests
by red routes of flame,
blinded by their luster,
blinded by their eyes,
like a sinister vulture of smoke
that plucks out the heart of flame.

Because rare metal or precious stone,
smooth as simple rock
shaping castles with the curve of dry cards
or by the sand of wrinkled breasts,
and the motherly humus of mined bones,

are all consumed with a gloomy crackle of
pleasure,
when the form in itself, pure form,
gives up to the joy of its own death
and in its thirst for consuming
it compresses to flames great lights,
the ritual oil of the senses,
that without lips, fingers, eyes,
if, step by step, death by death, crazy
taking refuge in its swollen grids,
it watches while each devourers the other,
animal to plant,
plant to stone
stone to fire,
fire to the sea,
the sea to clouds,
clouds to the sun
until all is a vast river
of cloudy semen that congeals
in an inaccessible tedium
with the lavish flow of its appetite.
It does not spit up from its guts an ounce,
for the silent arc of its fountains.
Between the glow of hidden lanterns
where nothing is coming or going,
where the dream does not reside,
where nothing or no one, never dies again,
there, alone, above great waters,
the Spirit of God now hovers

with a sound more than crying, yet crying,
as if wounded,--God also--irrelevant,
impaled by a hair,
by the almond eye of death
that emanates from His mouth, God
has finally drowned His own words.

ALLELUIA! ALLELUIA!

Knock, knock! Who is it?
It is the Devil, it is a durable weariness,
a desire to scatter these hostile chains,
this endless, stubborn dying.
This living death that kills.
Oh Lord, in your delicate handiwork,
in the rose and in the stone
in the various stars
and the flesh that is wasted
like a wild bonfire
in the song and in the dream
in the color of eyes, you are dying.

Knock, knock! Who is it?
It is the Devil, it is blind happiness,
a hunger to devour the air we breath
with my mouth, my eyes, my hands.
Those pungent spasms of ejaculation
in one burst of laughter,
ah this shameless, insulting death
that kills us from a distance

with the pleasure we take in dying,
by a cup of tea, by a mere caress.

Knock, knock! Who's there?
It is the Devil, it is the death of scratching
ants, that insult our dust--Oh lord,
perhaps they have killed you,
far away, hundreds of ages before.
Without telling us, crumbs, dregs,
ashes of you are still present
like a conjuring star.
By that starlight, by a hollow light
that reaches the world,
you hide your infinite catastrophe.

(Dance)

Out of my sleepless eyes
my own death is spying on me.
It looks at me, it charms me
with a lazy eye.
Come on you little bitch
with your frozen blush,
come on--to hell with it.

###

The Poetry of José Gorostiza

www.ingramcontent.com/pod-product-compliance
Ingram Content Group UK Ltd.
Pitfield, Milton Keynes, MK11 3LW, UK
UKHW041936190726
13854UKWH00004B/1618